SAND

BY HUGH HOWEY

Sand

Part I - The Belt of the Buried Gods

Copyright © 2013 by Hugh Howey

ISBN-13: 978-149375-100-6
ISBN-10: 1-493-75100-X

www.hughhowey.com

Give feedback on the book at:
hughhowey@gmail.com

Twitter: @hughhowey

First Edition

Printed in the U.S.A

For the stricken.

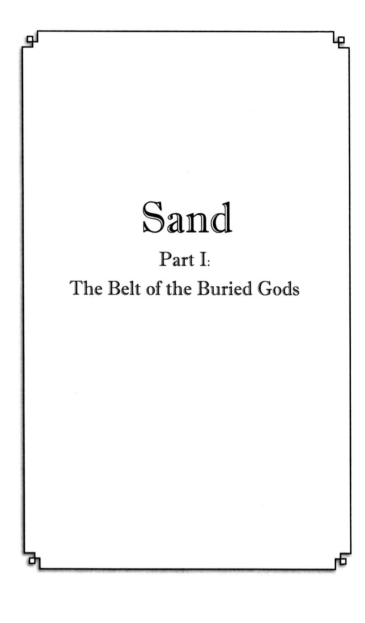

Sand

Part I:

The Belt of the Buried Gods

·1·
The Valley of Dunes

Starlight guided them through the valley of dunes and into the northern wastes. A dozen men walked single file, kers tied around their necks and pulled up over their noses and mouths, leather creaking and scabbards clacking. The route was circuitous, but a direct line meant summiting the crumbling sand and braving the howling winds at their peaks. There was the long way and there was the hard way, and the brigands of the northern wastes rarely chose the hard way.

Palmer kept his thoughts to himself while the others swapped lewd jokes and fictitious tales of several kinds of booty scored. His friend Hap walked farther ahead, trying to ingratiate himself with the older men. It was more than a little unwise to be wandering the wastes with a band of brigands, but Palmer was a sand diver. He lived for that razor-thin line between insanity and good sense. And besides, these braggarts with their beards and foul odors were offering a month's pay for two days of work. A hike into the wastes and a quick dive were nothing before a pile of coin.

The noisy column of men snaked around a steep dune, out of the lee and into the wind. Palmer adjusted his flapping ker. He tucked the edge of the cloth underneath his goggles to keep it in place. Sand peppered the right side of his face, telling him they were heading north. He could know without glancing up at the stars, know without seeing the high peaks to the west. The winds might abate or swell in fury, but their direction was as steady as the course of the sun. East to west, with the sand that rode along lodging in Palmer's hair, filling his ears, stacking up in curving patterns of creeping dunes, and burying the world in a thousand meters of hellish grit.

As the piratical laughter from the column died down, Palmer could hear the other voices of the desert chorus. There was the moaning of the winds, and a shushing sound as waves of airborne sand crashed into dunes and raked across men like gritpaper. Sand on sand made a noise like a hissing rattler ready to strike. Even as he thought this, a wrinkle in the dune beside him turned out to be more than a wrinkle. The serpent slithered and disappeared into its hole, as afraid of Palmer as he of it.

There were more sounds. The clinking of the heavy gear on his back: the dive bottles and dive suit, the visor and fins, his regulator and beacons, all the tools of his trade. There was the call of cayotes singing to the west, their piercing wails uniquely able to travel into the wind to warn neighboring packs to stay away. They were calling out that men were coming, couldn't you smell them?

Beyond these myriad voices was the heartbeat of the desert sands, the thrumming that never ceased and could be felt day and night in a man's bones, day and night from womb to grave. It was the deep rumbles that emanated from No Man's Land far to the east, that rolling thunder or those rebel bombs or the farting gods—whichever of the many flavors of bullshit one believed.

Palmer homed in on those distant grumbling sounds and thought of his father. His opinion of his dad shifted like the dunes. He sometimes counted him a coward for leaving in the night. He sometimes reckoned him a bold sonofabitch for setting off into No Man's Land. There was something to be said for anyone who would venture into a place from where no soul had ever returned. Something less polite could be said about an asshole who could walk out on his wife and four kids to do so.

There was a break in the steep dune to the west, an opening in the sand that revealed a wide patch of star-studded sky. Palmer scanned the heavens, eager to dwell on something besides his father. The ridgeline of the impassible Stone Mountains could be seen even in the moon's absence. Their jagged and daunting edge was marked by a black void where constellations suddenly ended.

Someone grabbed Palmer's elbow. He turned to find that Hap had fallen back to join him. His friend's face was underlit by the dive light dangling from his neck, set to dim.

"You aiming for the strong and silent type?" Hap hissed, his voice muffled by ker and wind.

Palmer hitched his heavy dive pack up his shoulders, could feel the sweat trapped between his shirt and the canvas sack. "I'm not aiming for anything," he said. "Just lost in thought."

"All right. Well, feel free to cut up with the others, huh? I don't want them thinking you're some kinda psycho or nuthin."

Palmer laughed. He glanced over his shoulder to see how far behind the next guy was and which way the wind was carrying their words. "Really?" he asked. "Because that'd be kinda boss, dontcha think?"

Hap seemed to mull this over. He grunted. Was probably upset he hadn't come up with it first.

"You're sure we're gonna get paid for this dive?" Palmer asked, keeping his voice down. He fought the urge to dig after the sand in his ear, knowing it would just make it worse. "I don't wanna get stiffed like last time."

"Fuck no, these guys have a certain code." Hap slapped him on the back of the neck, sand and sweat mixing to mud. "Relax, Your Highness. We're gonna get paid. A quick dive, some sand in our lungs, and we'll be sipping iced drinks at the Honey Hole by Sunday. Hell, I might even get a lap dance from your mom."

"Fuck off," Palmer said, knocking his friend's arm away.

Hap laughed. He slapped Palmer again and slowed his pace to share another joke about Palmer's mom with the others. Palmer had heard it before. It got less funny and grew more barbs every time. He walked alone in silence, thoughts flitting to his wreck of a family, the sweat on the back of his neck cooling in the breeze as it gathered sand, that iced drink at the Honey Hole not sounding all that bad, to be honest.

·2·
The Belt of the Gods

They arrived at the camp to find a tall fire burning, its beating glow rising over the dunes and guiding the men home in a dance of shadows. There were manly reunions of slapped backs and shoulders held, sand flying off with each violent embrace. The men stroked their long beards and swapped gossip and jokes as though they'd been apart for some time. Packs were dropped to the ground, canteens topped from a barrel. The two young divers were told to wait by the fire as some of the others ambled toward a gathering of tents nestled between steep dunes.

Palmer was thankful for the chance to sit. He shrugged off his dive pack and arranged it carefully by the fire. Folding his aching legs beneath him, he sat and leaned against the pack and enjoyed the flickering warmth of the burning logs.

Hap settled down by the fire with two of the men he'd been chatting with during the hike. Palmer listened to them argue and laugh while he gazed into the fire, watching the logs burn. He thought of his home in Springston, where it would be a crime to fell a tree and light it on fire, where coals of hardened shit warmed and stunk up homes, where piped gas would burn one day but then silently snuff out a family in their sleep the next. In the wastes, such things didn't matter. The scattered groves were there to be razed. The occasional animal to be eaten. Bubbling springs lapped up until they were dry.

Palmer wiggled closer to the flames and held out his palms. The sweat from the hike, the breeze, the thoughts of home had turned him cold. He smiled at an eruption of voices that bravely leapt through the tall flames. He laughed when the others laughed. And when his twisting stomach made noises, he lied and said it was because he was hungry. The truth was that he had a very bad feeling about this job.

To start with, he didn't know any of these men. And his sister had warned him of the savages he *did* know, much less those strange to him. Hap had vouched for the group, whatever that was worth. Palmer turned and watched his friend share a joke in the firelight, his face an orange glow, his arms a blur of enthusiasm. Best friends since dive school. Palmer figured they would go deeper for each other than anyone else across the sands. That made the vouch count for something.

Beyond Hap, parked between two steep dunes, Palmer saw two sarfers with their sails furled and masts lowered. The wind-powered craft rocked on their sleek runners. They were staked to the sand but seemed eager to race off somewhere, or perhaps Palmer was projecting. He wondered if after this job, maybe these guys would give him and Hap a ride back into town. Anything to avoid the night hikes and the bivouacking in the lee of blistering dunes.

A few of the men who had hiked with them from Springston dropped down and joined the loose circle around the fire. Many of them were old, in their late forties probably, more than twice Palmer's age and about as long as anyone was meant to last. They had the leather-dark skin of nomads, of desert wanderers, of gypsies. Men who slept beneath the stars and toiled under the sun. Palmer promised himself he would never look like that. He would make his fortune young, stumble on that one cherry find, and he and Hap would move back to town as heroes and live in the shade. A dune of credits would absolve old sins. They would open a dive shop, make a living selling and repairing gear, equipping the unlucky saps who risked their lives beneath the sand. They would see steady coin from the fools chasing piles of it. Chasing piles just as he and Hap were right then.

A bottle was passed around. Palmer raised it to his lips and pretended to drink. He shook his head and wiped his mouth as he leaned to the side to pass the bottle to Hap. Laughter was thrown into the fire, sending sparks up toward the glittering heavens.

"You two."

A heavy hand landed on Palmer's shoulder. He turned to see Moguhn, the black brigand who had led their march through the dunes. Moguhn gazed down at him and Hap, his silhouette blotting out the stars.

"Brock will see you now," he said. The brigand turned and slid into the darkness beyond the fire.

Hap smiled, took another swig, and passed the bottle to the bearded man at his side. Standing, he smiled at Palmer, an odd smile, cheeks full, then turned and spat into the flames, sending the fire and laughter higher. He slapped Palmer on the shoulder and hurried after Moguhn.

Palmer grabbed his gear before following along, not trusting anyone to watch after it. When he caught up, Hap grabbed him by the elbow and pulled him aside. Together, they followed Moguhn down the packed sand path between the firepit and the cluster of tents.

"Play it cool," Hap hissed. "This is our ticket to the big time."

Palmer didn't say anything. All he wanted was a score that could retire him, not to prove himself to this band and join them. He licked his lips, which still burned from the alcohol, and cursed himself for not drinking more when he was younger. He had a lot of catching up to do. He thought of his little brothers and how he'd tell them, when he saw them again, not to make the same mistakes he had. Learn to dive. Learn to drink. Don't burn time learning wasteful stuff. Be more like their sister and less like him. That's what he would say.

Moguhn was nearly invisible in the starlight, but came into relief against tents that glowed from the throb of flickering lamps. Someone threw a flap open, which let out the light like an explosion of insects. The thousands of stars overhead dimmed, leaving the warrior god alone to shine bright. It was Colorado, the great sword-wielding constellation of summer, his belt a perfect line of three stars aimed down the path as if to guide their way.

Palmer looked from that swath of jewels to the dense band of frost fire that bloomed back into existence as the tent was closed. This band of countless stars stretched from one dune straight over the sky to the far horizon. It was impossible to see the frost fire in town, not with all the gas fires burning at night. But here was the mark of the wastes, the stamp overhead that told a boy he was very far from home, that let him know he was in the middle of the wastes and the wilds. And not just the wilds of sand and dune but the wilds of life, those years in a man's twenties when he shrugs off the shelter of youth and before he has bothered to erect his own. The tent-less years. The bright and blinding years in which men wander as the planets do.

A bright gash of light flicked across those fixed beacons, a shooting star, and Palmer wondered if maybe he was more akin to this. Perhaps he and Hap both. They were going places, and in a hurry. Flash and then gone, off to somewhere new.

Stumbling a little, he nearly tripped over his own boots from looking up like that. Ahead of him, Hap ducked into the largest of the tents. The canvas rustled like the sound of boots in coarse sand; the wind yelped as it leapt from one dune to the next; and the stars overhead were swallowed by the light.

·3·
The Map

The men inside the tent turned their heads as Hap and Palmer slipped inside the flap. The wind scratched the walls like playful fingernails, the breeze asking to be let in. It was warm from the bodies and smelled like a bar after a work shift: sweat and rough brew and clothes worn for months.

A dune of a man waved the two boys over. Palmer figured him for Brock, the leader of this band who now claimed the northern wastes, an imposing man who had appeared seemingly out of nowhere as most brigand leaders do. Building bombs one year, serving someone else, until a string of deaths promotes a man to the top.

Palmer's sister had warned him to steer clear of men like this. Instead of obeying her, he now steered toward the man. Palmer set his gear down near a stack of crates and a barrel of water or grog. There were eight or nine men standing around a flimsy table set in the middle of the tent. A lamp had been hung from the center support; it swayed with the push and pull of the wind on the tent frame. Thick arms plastered with tattoos were planted around the table like the trunks of small trees. The tattoos were decorated with raised scars made by rubbing grit into open wounds.

"Make room," Brock said, his accent thick and difficult to place, perhaps a lilt of the gypsies south of Low-Pub or the old gardeners from the oasis to the west. He waved his hand between two of the men as though shooing flies from a plate of food, and with minimal grumbling, the two bearded men pressed to the side. Hap took a place at the waist-high table, and Palmer joined him.

"You've heard of Danvar," Brock said, forgoing introductions and formalities. It seemed like a question, but it was not spoken like one. It was an assumption, a declaration. Palmer glanced around the table to see quite a few men watching him, some rubbing their long and knotted beards. Here, the mention of legends did not elicit an eruption of laughter. Here, grown men looked at hairless youth as if sizing them up for dinner. But none of these men had the face-tats of the cannibals to the far north, so Palmer assumed he and Hap were being sized up for this job, being measured for their worthiness and not for some stew.

"Everyone's heard of Danvar," Hap whispered, and Palmer noted the awe in his friend's voice. "Will this lead us there?"

Palmer turned and surveyed his friend, then followed Hap's gaze down to the table. The four corners of a large piece of parchment were pinned down by meaty fists, sweating mugs, and a smoking ashtray. Palmer touched the edge of the parchment closest to him and saw that the mottled brown material was thicker than normal parchment. It looked like the stretched and tanned hide of a cayote, and felt brittle as though it were very old.

One of the men laughed at Hap's question. "You already *are* here," he roared.

An exhalation of smoke drifted across the old drawing like a sandstorm seen from up high. One of Brock's sausage fingers traced the very constellation Palmer had been staring at dizzily just moments before.

"The belt of the great warrior, Colorado." The men around the table stopped their chattering and drinking. Their boss was speaking. His finger found a star every boy knew. "Low-Pub," he said, his voice as rough as the sand-studded wind. But that wasn't the name of the star, as Palmer could tell him. Low-Pub was a lawless town to the south of Springston, an upstart town recently in conflict with its neighbor, as the two wrestled over wells of water and oil. Palmer watched as Brock traced a line up the belt, his fingertip like a sarfer sailing the winds between the two towns and across all that contested land. It was a drawn-out gesture, as though he were trying to show them some hidden meaning.

"Springston," he announced, pausing at the middle star. Palmer's thought was *Home*. His gaze drifted over the rest of the map, this maze of lines and familiar clusters of stars, of arrows and hatch marks, of meticulous writing built up over the years in various fades of ink, countless voices marked down, arguing in the margins.

The fat finger resumed its passage due north—if those stars really might be taken to represent Low-Pub and Springston.

"Danvar," Brock announced, thumping the table with his finger. He indicated the third star in the belt of great Colorado. The map seemed to suggest that that the buried world of the gods was laid out in accordance with their heavenly stars. As if man were trapped between mirrored worlds above and below. The tent swayed as Palmer considered this.

"You've found it?" Hap asked.

"Aye," someone said, and the drinking and smoking resumed. The curled hide of a map threatened to roll shut with the rise of a mug.

"We have a good guess," Brock said in that strange accent of his. "You boys will tell us for sure."

"Danvar is said to be a mile down," Palmer muttered. When the table fell silent, he glanced up. "Nobody's ever dove half of that."

"Nobody?" someone asked. "Not even your sister?"

Laughter tumbled out of beards. Palmer had been waiting for her to come up.

"It's no mile down," Brock told them, waving his thick hand. "Forget the legends. Danvar is here. More plunder than in all of Springston. Here lies the ancient metropolis. The three buried towns of this land are laid out according to the stars of Colorado's belt." He narrowed his eyes at Hap and then Palmer. "We just need you boys to confirm it. We need a real map, not this skin."

"How deep are we talking?" Hap asked.

Palmer turned to his friend. He had assumed this had already been discussed. He wondered if the wage he'd been promised had been arrived at, or if his friend had just been blowing smoke. They weren't here for a big scavenge; they were here to dive for ghosts, to dig for legends.

"Eight hundred meters."

The answer quieted all but the moaning wind.

Palmer shook his head. "I think you vastly overestimate what a diver can—"

"We dug the first two hundred meters," Brock said. He tapped the map again. "And it says here on this map that the tallest structures rise up another two hundred fifty."

"That leaves . . ." Hap hesitated, waiting no doubt for someone else to do the math.

The swinging lamp seemed to dim, and the edges of the map went out of focus as Palmer arrived at the answer. "Three hundred fifty meters," he said, feeling dizzy. He'd been down to two fifty a few times on twin bottles. He knew people who'd gone down to three. His sister, a few others, could do four—some claimed five. Palmer hadn't been warned they were diving so deep, nor that they were helping more gold-diggers waste their time looking for Danvar. He had feared for a moment there that they were working for rebels, but this was worse. This was a delusion of wealth rather than power.

"Three fifty is no problem," Hap said. He spread his hands out on the map and leaned over the table, making like he was studying the notes. Palmer reckoned his friend was feeling dizzy as well. It would be a record for them both.

"I just wanna know it's here," Brock said, thumping the map. "We need exact coordinates before we dig any more. The damn hole we have here is a bitch to maintain."

There were grumbles of agreement from the men that Palmer figured were doing the actual digging. One of them smiled at Palmer. "Your mum would know something about maintaining holes," he said, and the grumbles turned into laughter.

Palmer felt his face burn. "When do we go?" he shouted over this sudden eruption.

And the laughter died down. His friend Hap turned from the dizzying map, his eyes wide and full of fear, Palmer saw. Full of fear and with a hint of an apology for bringing them this far north for such madness, a glimmer in those eyes of all the bad that was soon to come.

·4·
The Dig

P almer lay awake in a crowded tent that night and listened to the snores and coughs of strangers. The wind howled late and brought in the whisper of sand, then abated. The gradual glow of morning was welcome, the tent moving from dark to gray to cream, and when he could no longer lie still and hold his bladder, Palmer squeezed out from between Hap and the canvas wall, collected his bag and boots, and slipped outside.

The air was still crisp from a cloudless night, the sand having shucked off the heat soaked up the day before. Only a few stars clung to the darkness in the west. Venus stood alone above the opposite dunes. The sun was up somewhere, but it wouldn't show itself above the local dunes for another hour.

Before it could beat down between the high sands, Palmer hoped to be diving. He relished the coolness of the deep earth, even the pockets of moist sand that made for difficult flow. Sitting down, he upturned his boots and clopped the heels together, little pyramids of scoop[1] spilling out. Slapping the

---

1 Sand that collects in boots.

bottoms of his socks, he pulled the boots back on and laced them up securely, doubling the knot. He was eager to attach his fins and get going.

He checked his dive pack and went over his gear. One of the prospectors emerged from the tent, cleared his throat, then spat in the sand near enough to Palmer for it to register but far enough away that he couldn't be certain if it was directed at him. After some consideration, and while the man urinated on the wall of a dune, Palmer decided this ephemeral range of questionable intent was between four and five feet. It felt scientific.

A wiry man with charcoal skin emerged from Brock's tent: Moguhn, who looked less fearsome in the wan daylight. He had to be Brock's second-in-command, judging by the way the two men conferred the night before. Moguhn lifted his eyebrows at Palmer as if to ask whether the young man was up to the day's challenge. Palmer dipped his chin in both greeting and reply. He felt great. He was ready for a deep dive. He checked the two large air bottles strapped to the back of his dive pack and took a series of deep and rapid breaths, prepping his lungs. There was no pressure to get all the way down to the depths Brock was asking. His dive visor could see through a couple hundred meters of sand. All he had to do was go as deep as he could, maybe clip three hundred for the first time, record whatever they could see, and then come back up. They couldn't ask more of him than that.

Hap emerged from the tent next and shielded his eyes against the coming dawn. He looked less prepared for a deep dive, and Palmer thought of the people he'd known who had gone down into the sand, never to be seen again. Could they feel it in the morning when they woke up? Did their bones know that someone would die that day? Did they ignore that feeling and go anyway? He thought of Roman, who had gone down to look for water outside of Springston, never to be found and never to return. Maybe Roman knew that he shouldn't go, had felt it right at the last moment, but had felt committed, had shaken off the nag tugging at his soul. Palmer thought maybe that's what he and Hap were doing at that very moment. Moving forward, despite their doubts and trepidations.

Neither of them spoke as they checked their gear. Palmer produced a few strips of snake jerky from his pack, and Hap accepted one. They chewed on the spicy meat and took rationed sips from their canteens. When Moguhn said it was time to go, they repacked their dive bags and shrugged on the heavy packs.

These men claimed to have dug down two hundred meters to give them a much-needed boost. Palmer had seen efforts such as these, and every diver knew to choose a site as deep as possible between slow marching dunes—but two hundred meters? That was deeper than the well in Springston his baby brother hauled buckets out of every day. It was hard to move that much sand and not have it blow back in. Sand flowed too much for digging holes. The wind had many more hands than those who pawed at the earth. The desert buried even those things built *atop* the sand, much less those made below. And here he and Hap were banking on pirates to keep the roof clear for them.

If his sister were there, she would slap him silly and haul him over hot dunes by his ankles for getting into this mess. She would kill him for getting involved with brigands at all. That, coming from someone who dated their kind. But then, his sister was full of hypocrisy. Always telling him to question authority, as long as it wasn't hers.

"That all your stuff?" Moguhn asked, watching them. He kept his black hands tucked into the sleeves of his white garb, which he wore loose like a woman's dress. Stark and brilliantly bright, it flowed around his ankles and danced like the heat. Palmer thought he looked like the night shrouded in day.

"This is it," Hap said, smiling. "Never seen a sand diver before?"

"I've seen plenty," Moguhn said. He turned to go and waved for the boys to follow. "The last two who tried this had three bottles apiece. That's all."

Palmer wasn't sure he'd heard correctly. "The last two who tried this?" he asked. But Moguhn was sliding past the tents and between the dunes, and he and Hap with their heavy packs had to work to catch up.

"What did he say?" Palmer asked Hap.

"Focus on the dive," Hap said grimly.

The day was young and the desert air still cool, but the back of his friend's neck shone with perspiration. Palmer shrugged his pack higher and marched through the soft sand, watching it stir into a low cloud as the first morning breeze whispered through the dunes.

Once they were past the gathering of tents, Palmer thought he heard the throaty rattle of a motor in the distance. It sounded like a generator. The dunes opened up and the ground began to slope down, the piles of sand giving way to a wide vista of open sky. Before them loomed a pit greater than the waterwell back in Shantytown. It was a mountain in reverse, a great upside-down pyramid of missing earth, and in the distance, a plume of sand jetted out from a pipe and billowed westward with the prevailing winds.

There were men down the slope, already working. Had to be a hundred meters down to the bottom. It was only half of what they'd been promised, but the scale of the job out here in the middle of the wastes was a sight to behold. Here were pirates with ambition, who could organize themselves for longer than a week at a time. The great bulk of the man responsible, Brock, was visible down at the bottom of the pit. Palmer followed Moguhn and Hap down the sand-slope, plumes of avalanche rushing before them, which the men at the bottom looked at with worry as it tumbled their way.

As Palmer reached the bottom, the sound of the blatting generator faded. He pulled his boots out of the loose and shifting sand, had to do so over and over, and saw that the others were standing on a sheet of metal. The platform was difficult to see, as it was dusted from the sand kicked loose by the traffic. Palmer didn't understand how the pit existed at all, what was causing the plume he had seen, how this was being maintained. Hap must've been similarly confused, for he asked Brock how this was possible.

"This ain't the half of it," Brock said. He motioned to two of his men, who bent and swept sand from around their feet. Palmer was told to step back as someone lifted a handle. There was a squeal from rusted and sand-soaked hinges as a hatch was lifted. Someone aimed a light down the hatch, and Palmer saw where the other hundred meters lay.

A cylindrical shaft bored straight down through the packed earth. One of the men uncoiled a pair ropes and began flaking them onto the sand. Palmer peered into the fathomless black hole beneath them, that great and shadowy depth, and felt his knees grow weak.

"We ain't got all day," Brock said, waving his hand.

One of his men came forward and pulled the ker down from his mouth. He helped Hap out of his backpack and started to assist with his gear, but Hap waved the old man off. Palmer shrugged his own pack off but kept an eye on the man. His beard had grown long, wispy, and gray, but Palmer thought he recognized him to be Yegery, an old tinkerer his sister knew.

"You used to have that dive shop in Low-Pub," Palmer said. "My sister took me there once. Yegery, right?"

The man studied him for a moment before nodding. When he moved to help Palmer unpack his gear, Palmer didn't stop him. He couldn't believe Yegery was this far north, way out in the wastes. He forgot the dive for a moment and watched old and expert hands handle his dive rig, checking wires and valves, inspecting air bottles that Palmer had roughened with sandpaper to add the appearance of more dives to his credit.

He and Hap stripped down to their unders and worked their way into their dive suits, keeping the wires that ran the length of the arms and legs from tangling. Palmer's sister had told him once that Yegery knew more about diving than any ten men put together. And here he was, licking his old fingers and pinching the battery terminals on Palmer's visor before switching the headset on and off again. Palmer glanced up at Brock and marveled at what these brigands had brought together. He had underestimated them, thought them to be disorganized and wishful treasure-seekers. He hoped they weren't the only ones that day who might more than live up to expectations.

"The hatch keeps the sand out of the hole," Yegery said, "so we'll have to close it behind you." He looked from Hap to Palmer, made sure both of them were listening. "Watch your air. We had a ping from something hard about three hundred or so down, small but steady."

"You can probe that deep?" Hap asked. He and Palmer were nearly suited up.

Yegery nodded. "I've got two hundred of my dive suits wired up here. That's what's holding the shaft wall together and softening the sand outside it so we can pump it out. We've got a few more days of fuel left in the genny, but you'll be dead or back by then."

The old tinkerer didn't smile, and Palmer realized it wasn't a joke. He pulled his visor on but kept the curved screen high up on his forehead so he could see. He hung his dive light around his neck before attaching his fins to his boots. He would leave the gear bag and his clothes behind, but he strapped his canteen tight to his body so it wouldn't drag—he didn't trust these men not to piss in it while he was gone.

"The other two divers," he asked Yegery. "What happened to them?"

The old dive master chewed on the grit in his mouth, the grit that was in all of their mouths, that was forever in everyone's mouths. "Worry on your own dive," he advised the two boys.

·5·
The Dive

The ropes pinched Palmer's armpits as he was lowered down the shaft. He descended in jerks and stops, could feel the work of the men above handling the rope with their gloved hands. The dive light illuminated the smooth walls of the shaft as he spun lazily this way and that. Hap drifted a few meters below him on his own line.

"It's fucking quiet," Hap said.

Palmer added to that quietude. He reached out and touched the wall of this unnatural shaft and felt with his fingers the unmistakable packed grit of stonesand[2]. This shaft had been made. A chill spread across his flesh. He remembered Yegery saying something about two hundred suits. "They created this," he whispered.

He and Hap inched downward, spinning as they went.

"They're using vibes to hold this together. And to loosen the sand before they pump it." Palmer remembered the soft and slushy feel of the sand as they had worked their way down the crater.

---

2   Sand held rigid by a dive suit.

"The bottom's coming up," Hap announced. "I can see the sand down there."

Palmer imagined the generator shutting off, or someone killing the power that held back this wall of sand, and all of it collapsing inward in an instant. It became difficult to breathe, thinking about the press of earth. He nearly turned his dive suit on, just in case.

"I'm down," Hap said. "Watch your fins."

Palmer felt Hap's hand on his ankle, steering him so he wouldn't land on top of his partner's head. The shaft was tight with the two of them on the ground. They worked the knots around their chests loose and tugged twice on the ropes like Brock had said. "I'll take lead," Hap offered. He pulled his regulator from his chest, checked the line, then reached over his shoulder to spin the air valve. He made sure it was locked before biting down on his regulator.

Palmer was busy doing the same. He placed his regulator between his teeth and nodded. Somehow, an odd calmness overcame him as he pulled that first deep breath from his bottle. Soon, he would be beneath the sand, the only place he had ever felt at peace, and all of this craziness around him would be forgotten. It would be just him and the depths, the calm cool sand, and the chance, however crazy, of discovering Danvar deep beneath their fins.

Hap powered on his suit by slapping the large button on his chest. Standing this close, Palmer could feel the vibrations in the air. They both set their homing beacons on the sand and turned them on. Palmer reached to his own chest and turned on his suit, then folded the leather flap over the switch so the journey through the sand couldn't accidentally shut it off and trap him.

Hap pulled his visor down over his eyes, smiled, and waved one last time. And then the sand loosened around his feet and seemed to suck him downward—and Hap disappeared.

Palmer turned off his dive light to save the juice. He pu
his visor down and switched the unit on. The world went black,
then gelled into a purplish blotch of shifting shapes. The air
screwed with the sandsight, making it impossible to see. With
the visor's headband pressed to his temples, Palmer thought
about what he wanted the sand to do, and it obeyed. The
suit around him vibrated outward, sending subsonic waves
trembling through molecules and atoms, and sand began to
move. It began to act like water. It flowed around him, and
down Palmer went.

Once the sand enveloped him, Palmer felt the exhilaration
a dune-hawk must feel in flight, a sense of weightlessness
and liberation, the power to glide any direction he liked. He
directed his thoughts like his sister had taught him so many
years ago, loosening sand below and pressing with a hardening
of sand from above, keeping a pocket loose around his chest
so he could breathe, diverting the weight of the earth around
him to hold back the pressure, and taking calm sips from his
regulator to conserve his air.

The wavering purple splotches were replaced with a
rainbow of colors, the cool purples and blues of anything far
away, bright orange and red for anything hard or close by.
Glancing up, the shaft above him glowed bright yellow. It
glowed like only the sand hardened by a suit could glow. It
was so bright that the white pulsing of the transponders was
difficult to spot, but one beacon was as good as any other.
He looked down and found Hap, a spot of orange with green
edges. His new visor worked great, had a much better seal to
keep the sand out and far better fidelity than his last pair. He
could clearly make out Hap's arms and legs where once he
would've seen a single blotch. Diving down after his friend,
he spoke in his throat to let Hap know he had a visual on him.

I hear you, Hap responded. The sound came from behind
and below Palmer's ears, vibrating in his jawbone. The two

Two hundred and fifty meters. Palmer felt a surge of pride. He couldn't wait to tell Vic—

Shit. Shit. Shit.

The words rattled through his teeth—Hap must be shouting in his throat. Palmer looked down at his friend, and then he saw it too. A bright patch. Something hard. Something *huge*.

Where's the ground? Palmer asked.

No fucking clue. What is that?

Looks like a cube. Maybe a house? Quicksand got it?

Quick don't go this deep. Fuck, it goes down and down.

Palmer could see that now. The square of bright red glowed into orange as they got closer, and he could see how the hard edges of the structure faded through to greens and blues as it went down. It was a square shaft of some sort, buried beneath the sand, sitting vertical and massive and deep.

Getting hard to breathe, Hap said.

Palmer felt it as well. He thought it was this strange object in his sandsight making it difficult to breathe, but he could feel how much more packed the sand was, how much harder to make it flow. He could still sink, but rising up would be a test. The weight of all that sand above him could be keenly felt.

We turn back? Palmer asked. His goggles said two fifty. It was another fifty or so down to the structure. With the two hundred meters they'd cheated from the dig, they were technically at four fifty right then. *Damn.* He had never dreamed of diving so deep. Only two fifty of it was him, he reminded himself. But still, his sister had told him he wasn't ready to go even that far. He had argued with her, but now he believed. Goddamn, was she ever wrong about anything?

Gotta see what it is, Hap said. *Then we go back.*

The ground must be a mile deep. Don't see an end.

I see something. More of these.

Palmer wished he had Hap's visor. His own was digging into his face, pushing on his forehead and cheekbones like it might smash right through his skull. He worked his jaw to lessen the pain, strained downward, and then he saw something too. Bright blues down there, more square shafts, and another to the side a little deeper, just a purple outline. And was that the ground down there? Maybe another three hundred meters down?

I'm getting a sample, Hap said. His words came in loud. The sand was dense, the visor bands transmitting the words from throat to jawbone louder than usual. Palmer remembered Vic telling him about this. He tried to remember what else he'd heard about the deep sand. He was sucking so hard to get a breath now that it felt like his tank was empty, but the gauge was still in the green. It was just the tightness around his chest, which was growing unbearable. It felt like a rib might snap. He'd seen divers taped up before. Seen them come up with blood trailing from their noses and ears. He concentrated. Told the sand to flow. He followed Hap, when his every impulse was to get out of there, to turn and find his beacon, to push the sand up as hard and as fast as he could, pile of coin be damned.

Hap reached the structure. The walls appeared perfectly smooth. A building. Palmer could see it now—an impossibly tall building with small details on the roof, some so hard and bright that they must be solid metal. A fortune in metal. Machines and gizmos. Something that looked like ducting, like the building used to *breathe*. This was not built by man, not by any man Palmer knew. This was Danvar of legends. Danvar of old. The mile-deep city, found by a bunch of smelly pirates, Palmer thought. And discovered by *him*.

·6·
Danvar

Hap reached the building before Palmer. It was a sandscraper that put all the sandscrapers of Springston to shame, could swallow all of them at once the way a snake could eat a fistful of worms. The top was studded with goodies, bright blooming flashes of metal untouched by scavengers: threads of pipe and wire and who knew what else. Palmer could feel his skin crawl, even with the sand pressing him so tight.

I'm taking a sample, Hap said.

Normally they would grab something loose from the ground, an artifact or scrap of metal, and rise up with it. Palmer pushed deeper and watched Hap scan the vast landscape of the building's roof. The adrenaline and the sight of such riches made it a little easier to move the sand—the sudden rush of willpower and desire helped—but breathing had become an effort.

Nothing loose, Hap complained, exploring the roof. The top of the building had to be as large as four blocks of Springston.

I'll break something free, Palmer said. He was now as low as Hap. Lower. His competitive spirit had driven him down past the edge of the building, dipping well past three hundred meters. The concept of breaking a personal record was lost in the rush of such a discovery. Such a monumental discovery. He worried no one would believe them, but of course their goggles would record everything. They would store the entire dive, would map the shapes beneath them, those great pillars reaching up like the fingers of a deity long buried.

And now the palm of this great god, the ground between the scrapers, was dimly visible. It was studded with bright metal boulders that Palmer recognized as cars, all preserved in great shape, judging by the signal bounce. But it was hard to read the colors this deep. He was in unfamiliar territory. As if to highlight this, the air indicator in his visor went from green to yellow. One of his tanks had gone dry, a dull click as a valve switched over. Not a problem. They weren't going any deeper. This was halfway. And he would use less air going up. Fuck, they were going to get out of here. They were going to do this. Just needed to look for something to break loose, a souvenir.

He probed for any sand that might be inside the building, sand he could grab and flow toward himself in order to breach the scraper and grab some small artifact. The flat wall before him had the signal bounce and the wavering shimmer of colors that screamed glass. *Hollow,* he told Hap. *I'm ramming it.*

Palmer formed a sandram with his mind, pictured a hardening of the sand in front of him and a loosening of the sand around that. His left hand twisted and turned inward the way it did when he concentrated, and he could feel himself sweating inside his suit despite the coolness of the deep sand. The ram was there. He made himself *know* the ram was there. And then he threw it forward, flowing the sand around it, losing control of the sand around his body for a moment, feeling it tighten everywhere at once like a coffin, his throat held fast by two great palms on his neck, chest wrapped with a wet and shrinking blanket, arms and legs tingling as the blood was cut off, and then the ram hit the building and dissipated, and Palmer had the sand flowing around him once again.

He took a deep breath. Another. It felt like pulling air through a narrow straw. But the flashes of light in his vision stopped their blinking. Palmer sank a little, but finally he righted himself. The view before him had changed. There was sand inside the building now. He had shattered the glass. A wavering patch of purple told him that there was air in there. A hollow. Artifacts.

I'm going in, he told Hap.

I'm going in, he told himself.

And then the sandscraper swallowed him.

·7·
A Burial

For as long Palmer could remember, he'd dreamed of being a diver, dreamed of entering the sand—but he had since learned that it was the *exiting* that took practice. A diver quickly learns a dozen flashy ways to get into a dune, each more spectacular than the last, from falling face first into the sand and having it softly claim him, to jumping backward with his arms over his head and disappearing with the slightest of splashes, to having the sand grab his boots and spin him wildly on the way down. Gravity and the welcoming embrace of flowing sand made many a glorious entry possible.

Exiting required finesse. Palmer had seen many a diver come sputtering out of a dune, sand in their mouth and gasping for air, clamoring with their arms as they lost concentration and got stuck up to their hips. He had seen many more come flying out with such velocity that they broke an arm or smashed a nose as they came spinning back to earth. Boys at school tried flipping out of dunes to disastrous and often hilarious results. Palmer, on the other hand, tried always to aim for a calm and unspectacular arrival, just like his sister.

She told him the calm looked braver than the boast. Look like
a pro. Pretend that one of those ruined sandscraper lifts still
worked and was depositing him on the topmost floor. That's
what he aimed for. But that was not how he arrived just now.

This exit was more like being belched out from the sand's
unhappy maw. He was spat sideways through the small
avalanche that had slid inside the building and was ejected
into the open air.

Palmer landed with a thud and a crunch, first on his
shoulder, then sprawling painfully to his back, his tanks
jolting his spine. The swimming purples vanished as his visor
was knocked from his eyes. There was sand in his mouth, his
regulator half-out, his lungs emptied by the impact.

Palmer removed the mouthpiece and coughed and spat
until he could breathe again.

Breathe again.

The air was foul and musty. It smelled like dirty laundry
and rotting wood. But Palmer sat in the utter and complete
dark of eyelids squeezed tight on moonless nights, and he
took another cautious sip. *There's air in here,* he told Hap,
speaking with throat whispers, but of course his friend
couldn't hear him. His visor band had been knocked askew,
and anyway he was no longer buried in sand, had no way of
projecting his voice.

Shouting wouldn't do, either. Palmer fumbled for his dive
light and flicked it on. A world of the gods unfolded dimly
before him. He turned away from the avalanche of sand, which
seemed to writhe and creep ever inward as the deep dunes
snuck inside to seek solace from their own crushing weight.

The objects in the room were recognizable. Artifacts just
like those found beneath Springston and Low-Pub. Chairs,
dozens of them, all identical. A table larger than any he had
ever seen, big as an apartment. Palmer tugged off his fins and

set them aside. He lowered his air tanks to the floor and killed the valve, made sure he saved his oxygen. Powering down his suit and visor, he relished the chance to gather himself, to give his diaphragm a rest from the struggle of breathing against the press of sand, a chance for his ribs to feel whole again.

On a side table, his expert salvaging eyes spotted a brewing machine. The pipes were rusted and the rubber appeared brittle, but it would fetch fifty coin at market. Double that, if his brother Rob could get it working first. The brewer was still plugged into the wall as if someone expected to use it still. The fit and finish of everything in the room felt eerily advanced and ancient at the same time. It was a feeling Palmer got from all the relics and spoils of a dive, but here the feeling overwhelmed, here it hit him on an inconceivable scale—

There was a crash and the hiss of advancing sand behind him. Palmer startled, expecting the drift to crush the rest of the weakened glass and consume him with his visor up on his head and his suit powered down. Instead, there was a thump and a grunt as Hap tumbled into the room.

"Fuck—" Hap groaned, and Palmer hurried to help him up. Sand slid around their feet as it found its equilibrium. It was wet and packed enough that it wasn't free to flow inside and fill the room. Not immediately, anyway. Palmer had swum through enough smaller buildings in shallower sand and had seen what sand would do if given the time.

"There's air," Palmer told Hap. "A bit foul. You can take your visor off."

Hap stumbled around in his fins a moment as he regained his balance. He was breathing heavily. Wheezing and gasping. Palmer gave him a chance to catch his breath.

Once he got his goggles off, Hap blinked and scanned the room. He rubbed the sand out of the corners of his eyes. His gaze seemed to flit across all the coin stacked here and there in the shapes of ancient things. And then he found his friend's face, and the two of them beamed at one another.

"Danvar," Hap said, wheezing. "Can you fucking believe it?"

"Did you see the other buildings?" Palmer asked. He was out of breath as well. "And I spotted the ground another three hundred meters or so further down."

Hap nodded. "I saw. I couldn't have gone another meter, though. Fuck, that was tight." He held his goggles to his face for a moment, checking his readouts most likely, and frowned. Hap shrugged his tanks off.

"Don't forget to kill your valve," Palmer said.

"Right." Hap reached to spin the knob. There was sand stuck to his face and neck where he'd been sweating. Palmer watched his friend shake a veritable dune out of his hair. "What now?" he asked. "Do we poke around? You got dibs on the brewer?"

"Yeah, I already spotted the brewer. I say we check a few doors, catch our breath, and then get the fuck out of here. If we stay longer than two bottles should last, our friends up top might think we only made it as far as the *last* assholes, and then they'll close that tunnel on our asses. I don't think I have enough air to get all the way back to the surface without that shaft."

"Yeah . . ." Hap appeared distracted. He popped off his fins, shook the scoop out of them, and dragged his gear away from the drift invading through the busted window. "Good move popping through the glass like that," he said. "I just saw you disappear, but I couldn't see inside."

"Thanks. And this is good, catching our breath. It would've been tight getting back up. We can get our strength."

"Amen. Hey, did you happen to spot the other divers on the way down?"

Palmer shook his head. "No, did you?"

"Naw. I was hoping they'd stand out."

Palmer agreed. There was almost nothing more valuable to salvage than another diver. It wasn't just their gear—which could run a pretty coin—it was getting cut in on any bounties they had or wills they'd left. Every diver was afraid to some degree of being buried without a tombstone, and so the bone-bounties, as they were called, made every diver a comrade of the dead.

"Let's try those doors," Hap said, pointing at the double set at the far end of the room.

Palmer agreed. He got there first and ran his hands across the smooth wood. "Fuck me, I'd love to get these out of here."

"You get those out of here and you could fuck someone prettier than me."

Palmer laughed. He gripped the handle, and the metal knob turned, but the door was stuck. The two of them tugged, grunting. Hap braced his foot on the other door, and when it finally gave way, the both of them went tumbling back into the table and chairs.

Hap laughed, catching his breath. The door creaked on its hinges. And there was some other sound, a popping like a dripping faucet, like a great beam settling under some weight. Palmer watched the ceiling closely. It sounded like the scraper was adjusting itself, like its belly was grumbling around these new morsels in its gut.

"We shouldn't stay long," Palmer said.

Hap studied him a long while. Palmer could sense that his friend was just as afraid as he was. "We won't," he agreed. "Why don't you go first. I'll save my dive light in case yours burns out."

Palmer nodded. Sound thinking. He stepped through the door and into the hallway. Across from him, there was a glass partition with another door set in it, a spider web of cracks decorating the glass, the effect of the building settling or being crushed by the sand. There appeared to be a lift lobby on the other side of the partition. Palmer had been in a few lifts in smaller buildings, found them a good way to get up and down if a building was full of sand. The hallway he stood in extended off in both directions, was studded with doors. To his right, there was a high desk like some kind of reception area, but everything was so damn nice. He coughed into his fist. Hopefully the air here wasn't—

Behind him, the door slammed. Palmer whirled in panic, thinking the drift must've flowed into the room and pinned the door shut, burying their gear. But he was alone in the hallway. Hap was gone.

Palmer tried the door. The handle turned, but the door wouldn't push open. He could hear the rattle on the other side as something was pressed against the door.

"Hap? What the fuck?"

"I'm sorry, Palmer. I'll come back for you."

Palmer slapped the door. "Stop fucking around, man."

"I'll come back. I'm sorry, man."

Palmer realized he was serious. Lowering his shoulder, he slammed against the door, could feel it budge a little. Hap must've shoved a chair under the knob. "Open the goddamn door," he yelled.

"Listen," Hap said. His voice was distant. He was across the room. "I burned my air getting down here. One of us needs to go up and tell the others what we found. I'll get more bottles and come back, I swear. But it's gotta be me."

"I'll go!" Palmer shouted. "That's my air, man. I can make it back up!"

"I'll be back," Hap called out. Palmer could hear a faint hiss as valves were opened and a regulator was tested. *His* valves. *His* regulator.

"You motherfucker!" Palmer shouted. He tried the adjacent door, but it wouldn't budge. He went back to ramming himself against the first door. He jerked the handle toward him as tight as he could, then threw his shoulder into the wood, thought he felt the chair budge a little. Again and again. The door opened a crack. And then a gap. Enough to get his arm through. He reached inside and felt the rim of the chair, held it while he pulled the door shut tight against his arm, and the chair popped off the knob and went tumbling. Palmer shoved his way inside, banging his elbows on the two doors, swimming between those priceless walls of wood, tripping over the upturned chair, to see Hap still on the floor, tugging on a flipper.

Hap scrambled to his feet as Palmer raced around the table and past the long row of chairs. His friend lowered his visor down over his wide eyes, had a grimace of determination on his face as he staggered toward the slope of sand, running awkwardly in his fins, one of them flapping with its buckles loose.

Palmer ran and dove after Hap, who jumped headfirst into the sand. The drift gave way, absorbing him, but Palmer caught one of his fins. The sand was hard and unyielding; it knocked Palmer's breath out as he crashed into it. He looked down at his hands, at the flipper that had come loose. His friend was gone. And he had taken Palmer's air with him.

·8·
What Pirates Do

Hap kicked his way out of the building and into a wall of sand. So thick. He hadn't been prepared, felt like he was moving through mush[3]. He concentrated on the flow, tried to breathe, realized he had a fin missing. Goddamn. He was going to die out here. Die right on top of fucking Danvar.

He coaxed a sip of air out of Palmer's regulator. There was sand in his mouth. Hadn't had time to clear it off. Fuck, the look on Palmer's face. But what choice did he have? Stay down there and wait for Palmer to come back for him? Fuck no. Fuck that.

He loosened the sand above himself and kicked off the hard pack below. It was almost impossible to move his arms. He let the sandflow do most of the work, tried to remember all the older divers who laughed at noobs for using fins in the first place. It wasn't kicking, it was thinking that moved a man. That's what they said. He never believed them. He tried to now. He tried to breathe. So damn hard to breathe. Like a

---

3 Wet sand.

tourniquet across his chest, like his ribs were knitted together, like the whole world was sitting on him.

Up. He made the mistake of looking down, could feel the pull of gravity, the sucking of those purples and blues, that hard earth far below, fading now, becoming invisible, just a handful of buildings until there was only one, and then he kept his visor pointed up, looking for the blinking transponders, watching the gauge drop back to under three hundred meters. Two fifty. Hell yeah, a breath. He sucked on the tanks, was damn glad for Palmer's lungs for once, wasn't jealous in the slightest, and as he rose up and up, he felt that distance between him and his friend grow, that crushing depth, and some part of him knew, some dark sliver, that there was no going back. He had discovered Danvar. Him. It would be for some other asshole to risk his neck exploring it, pulling up all those artifacts. Hell, he hadn't even grabbed that brewer. Hadn't been any time. Breathing deeply now, sucking the tank down from yellow to red, he got under a hundred meters and no longer cared how much air was in the tank. He could get there. He could make it. The transponders above were blindingly bright. The orange and yellow glow of the shaft walls could be seen. Hap kicked straight for the white beacons and the soft bottom of the shaft, his legs sore, his ribs bruised from the effort, a joy in his throat—

Hap!

He heard the faint murmur in his jawbones. Palmer. Probably got his head in the sand, his visor on, holding his breath and yelling after him. Hap didn't answer, didn't raise the voice that happens in a man's throat when he whispers in his mouth, when he thinks aloud. He kept those thoughts to himself.

Hap, you fucker, get back here! Hap—!

Hap didn't hear the rest. His head broke through the bottom of that well. He lifted himself up clumsily, dragging his legs out of sand softened by the vibrations of his suit, until he was sputtering and balled up in the open air once more.

He spit out his regulator. The tanks were empty. Hap moved the visor up to his forehead and took a few deep breaths in the pitch black. He fought the temptation to whoop for joy, to whoop for surviving. The others would be waiting up on that metal hatch and might hear him. Act cool. Act like you've done this before. A fucking hero, that's what he was. A legend. He'd never pay for a drink in any dive bar for the rest of his life. He flashed forward to himself in old age, in his forties, weathered and gray, sitting in the Honey Hole with two girls on his lap, telling people about the day he discovered Danvar. Palmer would have some heroic role to play. He'd see to that. He'd have the bartender buy him another round so he could toast Palmer's name. And the girls . . .

With his dive light on and his suit off, he fumbled for one of the dangling ropes, knotted it securely under his arms, gave it three sharp tugs. Oh, the girls. He thought of the girls as the slack went out of the rope. Almost too late, he remembered the beacons, which weren't cheap, and reached for his. The rope caught and started lifting him. Hap yelled for them to wait and scrambled after Palmer's beacon, which was worth a good twenty coin. He got his fingers on it as the rope began to haul him up, clutched the small device in his palm. While they hauled him through the shaft, he kept his one flipper on the wall to keep him from bouncing around and tucked the two transponders into the belly pocket on his suit. Fuck. He'd made it.

••••

The disc of light above grew larger and brighter as Hap was pulled skyward. He could see the sun shining down from directly overhead, so it must already be noon. Damn. Had they been down there that long? Someone above him barked orders to the men handling the rope. He could hear men grunting as they took up the line hand over hand, lifting him in swaying jerks. When he got to the lip, Hap helped, grabbing the hot edge of the metal platform, feeling the burn through his gloves as he pulled himself up on weary arms, kicking with his feet.

Two of the pirates grabbed him by his dive suit and tanks and hauled him out.

"Where's your friend?" someone asked, peering over the lip.

"Didn't make it," Hap said. He tried to take deep breaths. The old man who had checked over Palmer's gear searched Hap's face for a beat, and then waved his arms toward the high dune where the generator could be heard and a plume of sand filled the sky. But Brock pushed the old man's arms down and glared up in the same direction, waving some command off. Soon, everyone was looking at Hap. The dive master studied the deep shaft as if hoping Palmer would appear.

"How far'd you get?" Moguhn asked, his dark eyes flashing. "What'd you see?"

Hap realized he was still out of breath from the excitement, the adrenaline. "Danvar," he wheezed, beaming with triumph. "Sandscrapers like nobody's ever seen." He looked to Brock, whose eyes shined bright. "Sandscrapers everywhere, hundreds of meters tall, like twenty or thirty Springstons put together. Artifacts all over the place—"

"You were down a long time on two tanks," the dive master said. "We'd almost given you up."

"We found a pocket of air in one of the tallest scrapers, so we looked around a bit." He tried to make it sound matter-of-course. "We wanted to get you your money's worth." Hap beamed up at Brock. All of this would go in his stories, all would be embellished over the years.

"Did you record it all?" Brock asked in that deep and guttural accent of his. "Did you get a map of the area? Precise coordinates? Everything has to be precise."

"It's all stored in my visor." Hap tapped the band pushed up on his head.

"Let's have them," Brock said, holding out his hand. Two of the other men were behind Hap, holding that large metal hatch open. Hap was about to say that he'd want to see the coin first when he felt his visor tugged off his head and handed over. It took him a pause to realize that Brock's command hadn't been directed at him at all.

"Thank you," Brock said. He smiled at Hap. "And now, I trust you can keep a secret."

Hap was about to answer, to tell him that he damn sure could, but he quickly realized that this wasn't directed at him either. This flash of understanding came right before Moguhn shoved him in the chest and Hap felt himself go backwards. He windmilled his arms, stirring the air, a grunt and a helpless squeak escaping his lungs, his heels rocking back dangerously, before he tumbled into the dark.

He hit the hard wall of that deep shaft and spun down, the air whistling past his ears, his stomach up in his throat and choking off his screams. He fell swiftly. Felt a dangling rope, and the wild swinging of his arms caught a wrap. A wrap on his wrist, catching tight, and then the sting, the burn, as it caught his weight and he slid down and down, the rope whistling as it rubbed his flesh, biting, on fire, cutting through his skin and sinking to the bone, tumbling and tumbling until he hit in an explosion of agony.

His leg, his back, the tanks, and then his head, so fast it was almost at once. He couldn't feel his body. *He couldn't feel his body*. His arm was in the air, hung up in the rope. By his dive light, he could see the rope buried deep in his flesh, squeezing bone, blood racing down to his elbow.

Hap tried to move, but he couldn't. Turning his head, he saw his boot near his shoulder. His boot was near his shoulder. And Hap realized, numbly and sickeningly, that his foot was still in it.

Oh fuck, oh fuck. His body was ruined. His mind was still aware, could see what had happened to him, and he knew it wasn't something he would ever recover from. He was an unnatural heap, but still alive.

Far above, shadows bent over the small disk of light. Hap tried to scream up at them, yell for help, yell a curse on them for all their days, but all that leaked out of him was a whimper, a rattle. One of the shadows moved, an arm waving, and some receding part of Hap's mind thought they were waving down at him. But they were waving beyond the rise of that great crater at whoever was holding the walls of that shaft open—because the power was killed, a connection severed, and those walls collapsed suddenly and all at once. And Hap's mouth, locked open in quiet agony, filled with sand. And the earth sat upon his broken chest.

Also by Hugh Howey

Molly Fyde and the Parsona Rescue
Molly Fyde and the Land of Light
Molly Fyde and the Blood of Billions
Molly Fyde and the Fight for Peace

The Hurricane
Half Way Home
The Plagiarist
I, Zombie

Wool Omnibus
Shift Omnibus
Dust

Coming Soon

Sand Part 2 - A Visitor (December 31st)
Sand Part 3 - Return to Danvar (January 15th)
Sand Part 4 - Thunder Due East (January 31st)

In the Air (A Wool Story) - June 2014
Peace in Amber - January 2014

About the Author

Hey. I'm the guy who wrote those books over to the left. I've been a vagabond most of my life. I lived on a sailboat, had a career as a yacht captain, then fell in love and settled down. But even domesticated, I've been moving about a lot. Two years in Virginia, five years in North Carolina, and now I'm back in Florida. I live in Jupiter with my wife Amber and our dog Bella. When I'm not writing, I'm usually walking Bella on the beach, snapping a photo or two, or sitting around with a good book.

You can follow me on Twitter: @hughhowey
Email me: hughhowey@gmail.com
Or catch up on the latest at: www.hughhowey.com

I have a newsletter at my website, and I rarely spam people.

Thanks for reading.
    -Hugh

CPSIA information can be obtained at www.ICGtesting.com
Printed in the USA
LVOW06s1218180114

369900LV00033B/287/P